Scarlett

PAPERCUTZ™

ARiOL Graphic Novels available from PAPERCUTZ™

ARIOL graphic novels are also available digitally wherever e-books are sold.

Graphic Novel #1 "Just a Donkey Like You and Me"

Graphic Novel #2 "Thunder Horse"

Graphic Novel #3 "Happy as a Pig..."

Graphic Novel #4 "A Beautiful Cow"

Graphic Novel #5 "Bizzbilla Hits the Bullseye"

Graphic Novel #6 "A Nasty Cat"

Boxed Set of Graphic Novels #1-3

"Where's Petula?" Graphic Novel

Coming Soon

Ariol #7 "Top Dog"

ARIOL graphic novels are available for $12.99 only in paperback, except for "Where's Petula?" which is $9.99. The ARIOL Boxed Set is $38.99. Available from booksellers everywhere. You can also order online from papercutz.com. Or call 1-800-886-1223, Monday through Friday, 9 - 5 EST. MC, Visa, and AmEx accepted. To order by mail, please add $4.00 for postage and handling for first book ordered, $1.00 for each additional book and make check payable to NBM Publishing. Send to: Papercutz, 160 Broadway, Suite 700, East Wing, New York, NY 10038.

ARIOL graphic novels are also available digitally wherever e-books are sold.

papercutz.com

Susan Schade and Jon Buller

New York

-for Henry August Kellert

Scarlett

Star on the Run

Created by Jon Buller and Susan Schade
Jeff Whitman- Production Coordinator
Bethany Bryan- Editor
Jim Salicrup
Editor-in-Chief

ISBN: 978-1-62991-291-2

Printed in China through Four Colour Printing Group
Printed November 2015 by Shenzhen Caimei Printing Co., Ltd.
Caimei Printing Building, Guangyayuan, Bantian, Longgang
Shenzhen 518 129

Papercutz books may be purchased for business or promotional use.
For information on bulk purchases please contact Macmillan Corporate and Premium Sales Department at (800) 221-7945 x5442.

Distributed by Macmillan
First Papercutz Printing

I

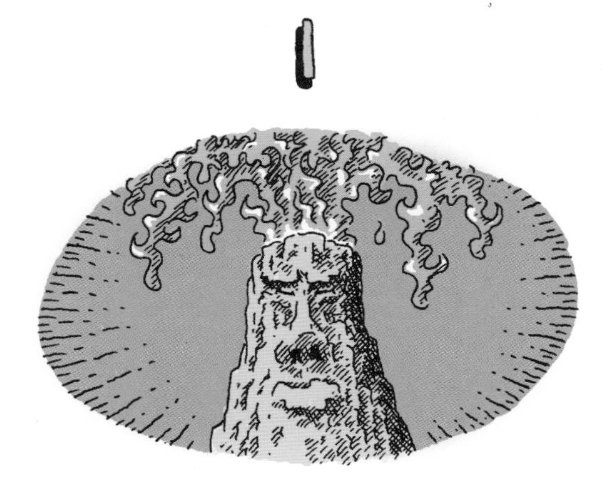

The Volcano

FLAMES SHOOT INTO THE EVENING SKY. THE VOLCANO GOD IS ANGRY.

HE MUST BE APPEASED! THE DRUMS BEGIN THEIR HYPNOTIC RHYTHM.
THUNKA
THUNK
THUNKA
THUNK

A LINE OF DANCERS EMERGES FROM THE HUT, CHANTING SOFTLY.
OOOOOAAAAAH

SCARLETT APPEARS ON THE PATH FROM THE SUMMIT.

SHE BEGINS HER DANCE.

THE OTHER DANCERS FORM A CIRCLE, AND SHE LEAPS INTO THE CENTER.

THE LAVA BEGINS TO FLOW...

SCARLETT PLEADS WITH THE VOLCANO GOD.
AAAAAOO

SHE STARTS TO SPIN!
OOAAAH

FASTER AND FASTER!
OOOOOOOO

SHE-
AAAAA
SPLAT

CUT!

YOU CLUMSY FOOLS! AGAIN! FROM THE TOP!

CAN'T YOU JUST CUT OUT THE PART WHERE I SLIPPED?

BACK TO THE PATH, SCARLETT! ROLL BACK THE ORANGE LAVA BLOB! PLACES, EVERYONE!

NO WAY! MY FEET HURT, AND I'M **TOO TIRED**!

SCARLETT, PLEASE DON'T DO THIS! YOU'RE HOLDING UP THE WHOLE FILM!

THE FILM CAN WAIT! RIGHT NOW I NEED SOME **REST** AND SOME **FOOD**!
SCARLETT

SOME WILD SALMON IN CATNIP CREAM SAUCE WOULD BE NICE.
SCARLETT

DON'T FORGET, IF IT WASN'T FOR ME AND MY LAB, YOU WOULDN'T EVEN **EXIST**, SCARLETT!
SCARLETT

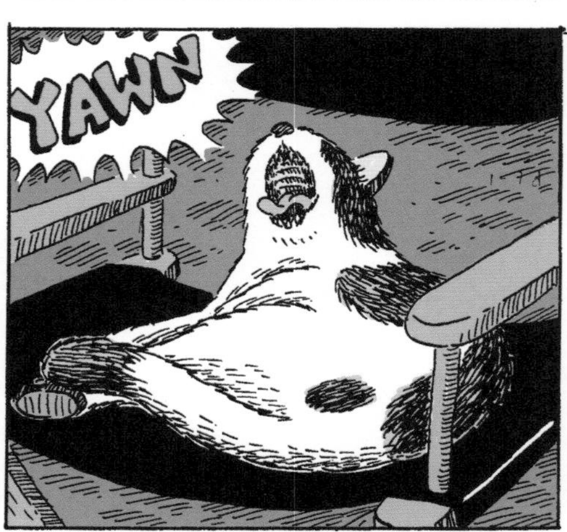
YAWN

ALL RIGHT, WE CAN KNOCK OFF EARLY TODAY, BUT TOMORROW YOU GET AN **ENERGY SHOT** BEFORE FILMING.
HANDLERS, TAKE THE ACTORS BACK TO THE LAB.
SCARLETT

YECHH!
I HATE THE ENERGY SHOT!

OH, NO! THEY'VE GONE BACK TO THE **FROZEN** SALMON!
SNIFF SNIFF

LET'S SEE WHAT'S ON T. V.
CLICK

I CAN'T TAKE ANY MORE BORING HUMAN REALITY SHOWS.

ZZZZ

GOOD MORNING, SCARLETT!

HERE'S A LITTLE SOMETHING TO **PEP YOU UP**!

COME HERE, LITTLE KITTY! HAHAHHH!

WHAT A HORRIBLE NIGHTMARE!

NOW I CAN'T SLEEP.
TO REC. ROOM

MAYBE I CAN GET UP A GAME OF DOMINOES.

HEY, TROTTER, ARE YOU IN THE MOOD FOR DOMINOES ?

NO THANKS, I WANT TO FINISH MY EXERCISE.

THIS PLACE BITES!

DID SOMEONE TURN ON THE AIR CONDITIONER?

THIS IS YOUR REC ROOM. PLEASE KEEP IT CLEAN.
THANKS,
PAFCO STUDIOS
?
SNACKS

PAFCO STUDIOS
SHIPPING AND RECEIVING
WHOA! I DON'T BELIEVE IT!
LABORATORY ENTRANCE

THIS WINDOW MUST HAVE BLOWN OPEN!

2

The Snow

Snow is *wet!*

I sank down in it almost up to my nose, and it made me gasp in surprise.

I thought I knew snow. Once, when I was a kitten, I had a bit part in a film about sled dogs. For the movie set, fluffy white flakes were released from the ceiling and drifted down to the floor where they covered the props in soft mounds. You could pounce in it and toss it around. It must have been fake! A lot of stuff in movies is fake, as I have since come to realize.

The *real* stuff is wet — yuck. And COLD! — like taking a bath in ice water. And I don't *like* baths. Not even when the water is warm.

After the first shock of it — the cold, the wet — I put it out of my mind. I needed to concentrate. I was on my own here.

I thought, *They might miss me at any moment!*

And I pushed off through the deep, wet snow.

In a few minutes I came to a place where the snow had been all smushed down by the tires of a large vehicle. I hurried along, crouching low in the rut in case someone was looking out of a window, trying to find me.

Then I heard a man's voice — "Same time again next week, Tim?" followed by the slam of a door . . . the start of an engine!

I panicked. Instead of hiding, I ran down the track as fast as I could go. I heard a truck coming behind me. It was too fast! I couldn't outrun it! It was gaining on me! I would be crushed in the road by the whirling tires!

But just as it reached my tail, the truck began to slow down. And I saw that the tracks were leading up to a gate — and the gate was wide open!

Once out of the gate, I leapt off the track into the deep snow and hid under a bush.

The truck roared through the gate and stopped, wipers flapping wildly back and forth across the slushy window. The driver jumped out to close the gate, then roared off again.

As the sound of his truck trailed off into silence, I waited. Nothing moved. No one made a peep.

I was *FREE!*

No more humans bossing me around; no more Sloan Pafco.

No more staring eyes.

No more people in white coats with needles and cameras, telling me, "Do this! Do that!"

No more cages and special diets!

Ha hah! I'm going to eat *MOUSE!*

Sneaking through the forest, I will hunt like a tiger . . . crouching . . . pouncing! Take that, you rodent! Munching and crunching. Yum.

I plowed my way onward through the snow.

I didn't know it would be so hard.

Big flakes fell from the sky, landing on my eyes and in my ears. I shook my head. I sat down in my own tracks and looked back, breathing hard.

The lab was nowhere in sight. The snow was filling in the marks I had left behind me. Soon there would be no sign of my passing. Good.

The tiger stands alone.

They'll never find me now, I thought.

On and on I trudged, until I could no longer feel my paws. They were like blocks of ice on the ends of my legs, so heavy I could hardly lift them to place one in front of the other. I stumbled. I got up.

I struggled on . . .

Maybe I wouldn't be a tiger, after all. Maybe I would be a HOUSE PET. *I will sit on a soft pillow and eat from a crystal bowl. I will have a cat door and go in and out at will. But I won't go out until it is warm. Then I will have a garden with a fountain and goldfish . . .*

The cozy little house before me was part of my dream. A house made of wood, with a roof over it, and a door where you could go in and get warm and some nice human would give you food — only a dream.

Or . . . I blinked and tried to focus my tired eyes . . . could it be real? I pushed on.

I can make it. I know I can make it. . . .

3

The Cabin

WHAT HAPPENED? HOW DID I GET HERE?

HE DRIVES THE LANE...

UH-OH! IT BOUNCES OFF THE RIM!
WHAT?

YOU CAN'T PLAY BASKETBALL, YOU LOUSY, NO-GOOD...

ACK!
CLUTCH

SLAM

HE'S STILL BREATHING.

WHAT'S THAT SMELL?

I'LL HAVE A QUICK LOOK AROUND WHILE HE'S SLEEPING.

HMM. I CAN SEE WHY HE SLEEPS OUT THERE ON THE FLOOR.

EL PRIMO RAVIOLI
EL PRIMO RAVIOLI

EL PRIMO RAVIOLI
EL PRIMO RAVIOLI

WHOOSH
EL PRIMO RAVIOLI
EL PRIMO RAVIOLI

EXCELLENT! I'M NOT LOCKED IN!
SLAM
EL PRIMO RAVIOLI
EL PRIMO RAVIOLI

I CAN LEAVE ANY TIME I WANT.

IF ONLY I COULD FIND SOMETHING TO **EAT.**

THAT'S INTERESTING!

I WONDER WHAT HAPPENS ON **FRIDAYS**.
FEBRUARY

A MOUSE!

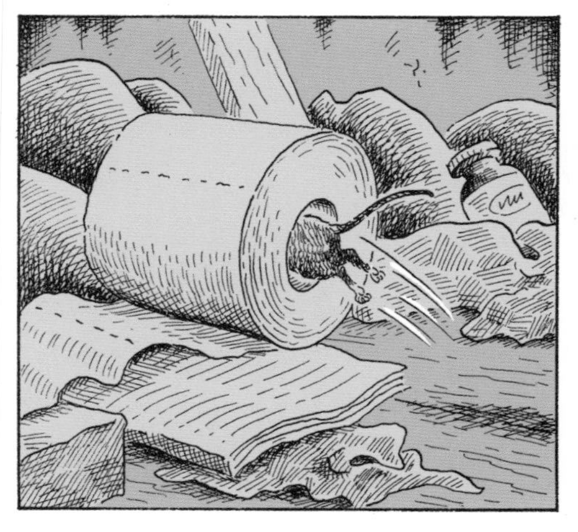

AH HA! I'VE GOT YOU NOW!

I DON'T KNOW. SOMETHING ABOUT ALL THAT **SKIN** AND **HAIR** IS MAKING ME LOSE MY APPETITE.

I'LL SAVE IT FOR LATER.

THE MAN CAN FEED ME WHEN HE WAKES UP.

THE REMOTE! I HOPE HE GETS ANIMAL PLANET!

NOW FOR A BREAKING STORY...
CLICK

SPYCAMS CONTINUE TO COMB THE AREA FOR SEVERAL ANIMAL ROBOTS THAT ESCAPED FROM PAFCO STUDIOS ON MONDAY.

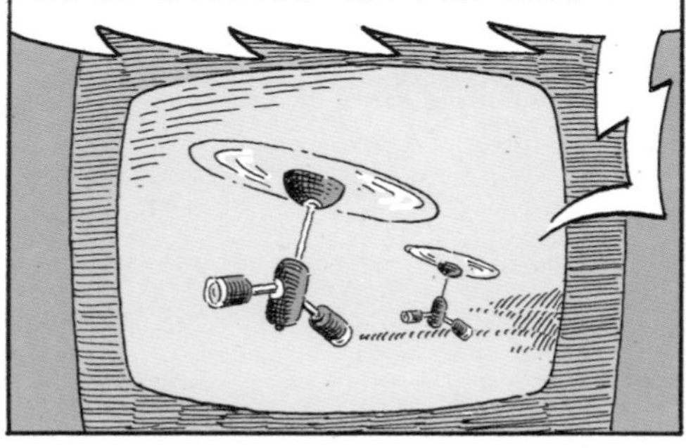

PAFCO STUDIOS! THAT'S **THE LAB!**

AREA RESIDENTS ARE ADVISED THAT, WHILE THESE ROBOTS MAY LOOK CUTE, THEY ARE **NOT REAL.** IF NOT HANDLED CORRECTLY, THEY CAN BE VERY DANGEROUS.

ROBOTS? NOT **REAL?** EXCUSE ME, I AM **NOT** A ROBOT!

HUH ?

WHO SAID THAT ?
COUNT IT, AND HE'S FOULED.
CLICK

WHO'S THERE ?

WHO'S THERE ? I SAID.

GET OFF MY PROPERTY!
EL PRIMO RAVIOLI
EL PRIMO RAVIOLI

4

The Man

He didn't see me!

He ran right out the door, leaving it wide open, and shouted, "GET OFF MY PROPERTY!"

I hid behind a smelly old sack.

Outside, in the silence of the snowy landscape, the sound of his angry shouts faded away to nothing.

"Nobody there," he muttered. "Guess I'm hearing things."

He came back in and shut the door.

"RAARK KOFF!"

He opened the door again and spit out into the snow. "HARUGH! Ptuii!"

Humans can be quite loud.

"Time for breffus," he muttered.

I came out of my hiding place.

That's more like it, I thought. It had been a long time since my last meal.

I looked up at him, waiting. *Would he like me? Would he feed me and let me stay? Or would he point his gun at me and chase me off his property?*

My heart pounded in my chest. He almost stepped on me, but I stood my ground.

He stopped just in time.

"A cat? Do I have a cat?"

"Mew?" I said.

"Oh, yeah, I remember now." He shook his head. "Out there in the snow. Thought you were a goner, Cat."

He reached for a can, a can opener . . .

Yes! I thought, and I hopped up onto the table.

"Do you like ravioli, Cat?" he asked me.

"I never had it before," I replied politely, "but I'll try anything. I'm starving!"

"Haha! I almost thought you said something. Here, Cat, fresh from the can."

He plopped a spoonful right onto the table in front of me.

I was so hungry, I didn't say anything about his table manners. I just dug in.

After I had taken a few bites, I licked my chops and said, "This ravioli isn't half bad."

The man stared at me for a few seconds.

"Oh, geez," he groaned, "now I'm hearing voices."

He spooned some of the ravioli into his own mouth and took the can to his chair. I followed, hoping for more.

"What're you lookin' at, Cat?" he said.

I said, "I have a name, you know. It's Scarlett."

"ANIMALS CAN'T TALK!"

A little shouting doesn't intimidate me.

"Yes, they can!" I said right back. "Look at Stuart Little!"

"Friend of yours?" he asked.

"No. He's a mouse. I'd like to eat him."

"TALKING MICE! Next thing you know, the chair will be telling me to sit someplace else. BURP!"

The man thumped on his chest with his fist, then he got up and took apart a plastic thing with a squiggly cord.

What's he up to, now? I wondered.

He punched at it with one fat finger, waited a few seconds, and said, "Hello, Walt's Grocery?"

Just as if it was a phone.

"This is Frank Mole, would you send over another case of canned ravioli?"

It *was* a phone! Come to think of it, I remembered seeing old phones like that on TV. The cord dangled around. I thought about biting it.

"And a case of cat food," I said loudly.

"And a case of cat food," he repeated into the old-fashioned phone. "And tell that kid to leave it outside the door. And no SNOOPING AROUND!"

The man shuffled back to his sagging chair and sank down in front of the TV with a long, wheezy sigh. "What's the score?" he said, turning up the volume.

"RESIDENTS WHO SPOT ANY OF THESE ANIMALS SHOULD CALL THIS NUMBER," said the TV.

Uh-oh. *Is this where the man figures out who I am and where I came from?*

"It's just a commercial," I said. "I wouldn't pay any attention to it."

"LOUSY ROTTEN COMMERCIALS!" he said.

The game droned on.

The man sank further into his chair.

Soon he was fast asleep. Rude noises came bellowing out of his open mouth.

Oh, well. What a day!

5

Spycams

NEXT MORNING-
CAT FOOD?

I DIDN'T ORDER ANY CAT FOOD!
CAT FOOD
RAVIOLI

I BELIEVE THAT'S FOR ME.

DO I REALLY HAVE A TALKING CAT, OR AM I IN WORSE SHAPE THAN I THOUGHT?
CAT
RAVIOI

I'D LIKE SOME NOW PLEASE.
I MUST BE LOSING IT.

SNIP
ON A CLEAN PLATE?

THANK YOU.

I'M GOING TO GET THE MAIL.

BUNCHA CRUMMY JUNK!

LET'S SEE... ELECTRIC COMPANY, WALT'S GROCERY, LUCKY MART... THAT SEEMS ALL RIGHT.

GOTTA PAY ON TIME OR THEY'LL COME AFTER ME.

WHO WILL COME AFTER YOU?
EVERYBODY!

THE **INSPECTORS!** THE **AUTHORITIES!** THE **TOWN!**

LET 'EM MIND THEIR OWN BUSINESS, AND STAY OUT OF MINE!

HAKHAK
HAKKH

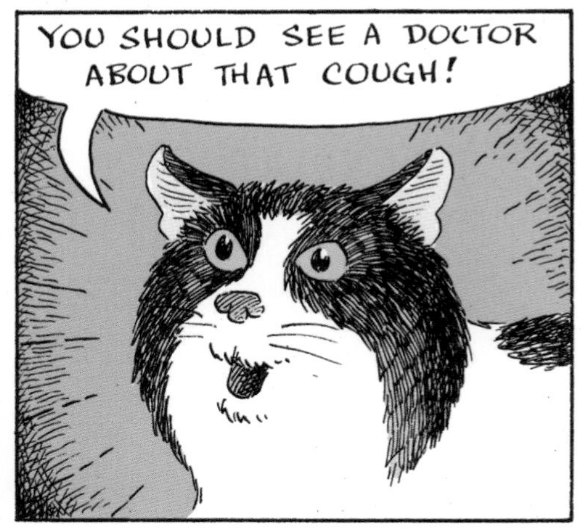
YOU SHOULD SEE A DOCTOR ABOUT THAT COUGH!

HAHA! THAT'S A GOOD ONE. LET ME TELL YOU SOMETHING, CAT—IF YOU WANT TO LIVE A LONG LIFE—

STAY AWAY FROM DOCTORS!

BRUSHA BRUSHA

SNIP SNIP SNIP

WELL, CAT, IT'S TIME TO CHASE THE DREAM!

I'M GOING TO BUY MY LOTTERY TICKET!

I HAVEN'T WON IN THREE MONTHS!

MAYBE IT'S TIME TO CHANGE MY **LUCKY NUMBERS!**
SCRAPE
SCRAPE

QUIK COPY
FAX 25¢
GIVE ME A LUCKY NUMBER, CAT.
HOW ABOUT TWENTY-FIVE?

HONK
TWENTY-FIVE ? GOOD ONE !
37FY
SOB

NOW GIVE ME ANOTHER NUMBER, CAT!
HONK
SCREEECH

37FY

THIRTY-SEVEN.

SPEED LIMIT 50
BOB
PUTT PUTT

SPEED
LIMIT
50

GOT ANOTHER ?
FIFTY.

LUCKY MART
25! 37! 50!
I LIKE IT!

STAY HERE. IF THEY SEE ME TALKING TO A CAT I MIGHT HAVE TROUBLE.

MART

THE SPYCAMS!

WINDOW
BZZZ

TROTTER! IS THAT YOU?

SCARLETT!

I JUST SAW SOME OF THOSE SPYCAMS!
I KNOW! THEY'RE AFTER ME. I HAVEN'T EATEN IN THREE DAYS.

QUICK! GET IN THE BACK OF THE TRUCK.
OOF!

HIDE UNDER THE TARP SO THEY CAN'T SEE YOU!
808

808

HEH HEH!
808

WE'RE GONNA BE LUCKY THIS TIME, CAT. I CAN **FEEL IT!**
LUCKY MART

6

Trotter

The spycams did not follow our truck. Why should they? Trotter was well concealed.

As we putt-putted slowly down the road, one shiny little car after another zipped past us.

I watched Frank Mole carefully. He turned the steering wheel this way and that and kept his eyes on the road.

When we pulled in next to the little house, he moved his foot over and pressed down hard on the small pedal, and the truck came to a stop. Then he turned the key, and the engine went quiet.

Very interesting. A cat on her own needs to learn as much as she can.

Frank pulled the key out of the hole.

"Got your ticket?" I asked him.

Frank quickly checked his pocket to make sure he still had his ticket. He looked at it and smiled. Then he climbed out of the truck and held the door open for me to jump down.

"Is it safe to come out now?" Trotter asked from under the tarp.

"YOW!" Frank jumped back. "Who's that? Get out of there! HIJACKER! THIEF! Get my gun, Cat!"

(As if I would get his gun! Even if I could.)

Trotter's nose was sticking out from under the tarp.

Frank's eyes bulged.

Trotter is a very handsome animal. Even tired and hungry as he was, with his fur all dirty and matted, you could tell he would play the leading dog.

"Have you got anything to eat?" he asked weakly.

"*HE* talks, too?" Frank whispered, shaking his head. "I don't believe it. Talking dogs! Talking cats! I must be losing my mind. *Voices! I'm hearing voices!*"

He suddenly sank down on his behind and sat there in the snow, holding his head.

I could tell he was in no condition to think for himself so I said, "Pull yourself together, Frank! Stand up!"

He stood up slowly.

"Good," I said. "Now open the back of the truck and let Trotter out. He's very tired and hungry."

With a dazed stare, Frank moved stiffly around to the back of the truck.

"And don't worry about what to feed him," I added. "He can eat ravioli for now — until we get some dog food delivered."

Frank rubbed his eyes. "But I don't have a dog," he grumbled.

"You do now," I said.

Frank opened the back of the truck and Trotter tumbled out.

"Let's get some food into you," I said, leading Trotter up to the door. "And snap out of it, Frank. Trotter is a very nice dog. You'll like him."

So Frank opened several cans of ravioli and dumped it on a plate.

Trotter wolfed it down. Then he fell into a deep, exhausted sleep.

"You better order the dog food now," I said to Frank.

He glared at me. "You can talk," he said. "Order it yourself!" (Frank seemed to be recovering from the shock of finding Trotter. He was getting his grouch back.)

"All right," I said, "if you give me the phone and punch in the number for me. What should I say?"

"Tell him to put it on my bill."

Frank put the phone on the shelf.

"You should get a cell phone," I said.

He grunted, then turned to the wall unit. "Five, five, five," he mumbled to himself, pressing each numbered button as he spoke. "One, eight, nine, two."

The phone was ringing.

"Walt's Grocery," someone said through the receiver.

"Hello," I said. *It was my first phone call ever!* "Is this Walt's Grocery?"

"I just said so, didn't I? Whaddya want?"

Walt is not very polite, I thought to myself. I said, "I'm calling for Frank Mole. He wants you to send over a case of dog food and put it on his bill."

"Frank's getting expensive tastes in his old age, isn't he? Ravioli not good enough for him anymore? Har, har, har!"

"It's for a *dog,*" I said in my snootiest voice.

"Just joking," Walt said. "Who're you anyway? Social worker?"

"I will be looking after Frank for a while," I replied. "That will be all, thank you." And I walked away from the phone. *Fresh!*

But I enjoyed making the call. *Five five five, one eight nine two, put it on Frank's bill, and I could order anything I wanted!*

After we had our own lunch, Frank looked at his clock.

"Almost lottery time," he said, rubbing his hands together. "And my numbers come from a talking cat! How can I lose? Even if it's nothing but a voice in my head. Must mean something."

So he still thinks I'm a voice in his head. Does he think the voice in his head just ordered dog food? Befuddled, that's what Frank is. Well maybe that's a good thing. I don't think he'll be turning us in to PAFCO Studios any time soon.

He turned on the TV and sat on the edge of his chair holding his ticket out in front of him to compare the numbers.

"C'mon, Lucky Cat," he grunted at the TV. "Don't let me down, now."

The TV announcer smiled at the viewers and said, "Today's winning triple play numbers are . . ." The numbers bounced up one at a time. "Twelve . . . three . . . forty-nine . . ."

Frank said a swear word and slumped back in his chair. His fist clenched around the crumpled ticket and he threw it on the woodpile. "Not even close," he muttered.

The TV droned on. Frank's head slipped sideways and he began to snore.

I watched him, wondering. Did Frank need that money so badly?

Frank has money in the bank. (I knew that much.) *That's why he can write checks to pay his bills.*

But where does he get the money to put in the bank? By winning the lottery? So, if he doesn't win . . .

Worrying about my future food orders, I hopped up on Frank's desk and began rummaging around . . . *bills paid, checkbook, bank statement, hmm . . . deposits — that's money coming in . . . balance — that's what's left. Why Frank has thousands of dollars! And money comes in every month, from somebody called Soc. Sec. There's nothing to worry about. I guess he just likes to win.*

Later, Trotter woke up and had a big drink out of the running faucet.

But Frank snored on.

"I don't like the look of him," I said to Trotter. "His bare skin is all pale and puffy-looking, like a muffin top."

"That's what humans are like," said Trotter. "It comes from having no fur."

"I don't know," I said. "And he doesn't breathe right – he *snorkles!* And sometimes he stops all together."

We watched Frank's heavy, irregular breathing for a few minutes.

Then Trotter said, "So are we going to live here, or what?"

"Well, it seems like a good place to hide out, for now anyway. Frank is very territorial. If anybody comes looking for us, he'll chase them off the property with his gun. I don't think we could do better."

I moved closer to the wood stove to get warm, but the fire wasn't putting out much heat.

"TIME FOR ANOTHER LOG!" I called loudly.

Frank didn't budge.

"Uh, are you talking to me, or him?" Trotter asked.

I looked him over.

"We need a log on the fire," I said. "Do you think you could take care of it?"

Trotter picked a log up with his teeth and tossed it on top of the stove.

"Nice try," I said, "But the log has to go *inside*. You have to open the

door . . . *HOT!*" I yelled as he reached for the stove door with his bare paw. "THE STOVE IS HOT! You have to use the special opener."

Trotter held the opener in his teeth and twisted the handle until the doors swung open. Then he pushed the log in, closed the doors by pushing on them with another log, and shut them up tight again by twisting the handle the other way. He may not be too bright, but I could see that he was going to come in handy.

"There's something I wanted to talk to you about, Trotter. It's worrying me.

"PAFCO Studios was on the TV news last night, about our escape and about the spycams. But it said we were *robots!* We *aren't* robots, are we? But if we aren't robots, why did they say we were robots? I mean, I know we're different from ordinary animals, but we're still *real,* right?"

Sometimes Trotter has this dumb look that makes me want to give him a good smack. Like now.

"Well?" I said. "Tell me we're real, Trotter. You don't feel like a robot, right?"

"Right," he admitted.

"And it hurts when you get a shot, right?"

"Right."

"And when you cut your foot, you *bled!* Robots don't bleed, right?"

"Unless they wanted to make robots that would bleed. You know, so they would seem more real."

I laid my ears back and narrowed my eyes. "That's not what I wanted you to say, Trotter."

"What did you want me to say?"

"That we aren't robots. That we're real."

"We aren't robots," he said. "We're real."

I turned my back on him and started washing.

"I mean it," he said. "I feel very real. I'm sure we're real. I just said what I said before for . . . for something to say. You know, to make conversation."

I sighed. "I'm sure we're real too. But we *are* different."

"Different, and better," Trotter said. "And I think we should stay here a long time. You found a good home for us, Scarlett."

"Let's nap," I said, curling up next to him. "Until dinner time."

7

Ambulance

SEVERAL WEEKS HAVE PASSED. FRANK HAS BECOME ACCUSTOMED TO SHARING HIS HOUSE WITH TALKING ANIMALS, ALTHOUGH HE IS STILL NOT SURE THAT THE VOICES AREN'T ALL IN HIS HEAD.
YOUR HANDWRITING IS GETTING WORSE AND WORSE. NOBODY COULD READ THAT.
THINK YOU COULD DO BETTER? ≡WHEEZE, HACK≡

YES! GIVE ME THAT PEN!

HMM. NOT BAD.

JUST LEAVE THE BILLS TO ME. TROTTER, CAN YOU HELP FRANK BACK TO HIS CHAIR?
HAK HAK

I NOTICED YOU DIDN'T EAT YOUR APPLESAUCE THIS MORNING!

DIDN'T YOU WATCH THAT PROGRAM ON PROPER NUTRITION?
NAG, NAG!

SEE THAT YOU PAY EVERYONE ON TIME, CAT! HAAK! HAAK!

I'M GOING OUTSIDE, SCARLETT. GOT TO TAKE A LEAK.

LOOK, SCARLETT, IT'S **WARM** OUT, AND THE SNOW IS FINALLY ALL GONE.

HEY, CLOSE THAT DOOR! I'M FREEZING! KAHAKKAK!

NEVER MIND, LEAVE IT OPEN. I HAVE TO BUY MY LOTTERY TICKET.

I'M WORRIED ABOUT HIM, TROTTER.
PUTT PUTT

LATER...
IT'S ALMOST DARK. FRANK SHOULD HAVE BEEN HOME HOURS AGO.
SHOULD I GO LOOK FOR HIM?

OK, BUT WATCH OUT FOR SPYCAMS.

A FEW MINUTES LATER...
SCARLETT ! COME QUICK!

HE'S IN HIS TRUCK AT THE END OF THE DRIVEWAY.

HE'S STILL BREATHING. I CHECKED.
808

WE NEED TO GET HIM BACK TO THE HOUSE.

THE MOTOR IS STILL RUNNING. I THINK WE SHOULD BE ABLE TO DRIVE THIS THING.

I'VE WATCHED HIM DO THIS. IT SHOULDN'T BE TOO HARD.

JUST TURN THE STEERING WHEEL IN THE DIRECTION YOU WANT TO GO.
OK.
808

SCARLETT! NOT SO FAST! STOP!
BOB

SKREEEEE
BOB

TRY TO GET HIM INSIDE.
I'LL GET A PILLOW.

FRANK, WAKE UP!

MAYBE WE SHOULD GET HIM SOME FOOD. THAT KUNG PAU CHICKEN THE OTHER NIGHT WAS VERY TASTY.

ALL YOU THINK ABOUT IS FOOD! I'M AFRAID THAT FRANK MIGHT **DIE**!

IF WORSE COMES TO WORST, I COULD DIG A BIG HOLE...
I'M CALLING 911!

BUT WON'T SOMEBODY COME?

THAT'S THE WHOLE IDEA. I'LL SAY I'M THE HOUSEKEEPER. WHEN THEY COME WE'LL ACT LIKE NORMAL PETS.

911.
I NEED TO REPORT AN EMERGENCY.

SHE SAID THEY'D BE HERE IN FIVE MINUTES.

SCARLETT, HOW DO NORMAL PETS ACT?

ACT DUMB AND WAG YOUR TAIL A LOT.— LIKE THIS...

HERE THEY COME.
EEEEEEEE

EMERGENCY SERVICES!
KNOCK KNOCK

HELLO?

HERE HE IS!

HANG ON, BUDDY! IT'S GONNA BE ALL RIGHT.

I WONDER WHAT HAPPENED TO THE HOUSEKEEPER?

UH...

OW!
WHAP

HOUSEKEEPER! DON'T MAKE ME LAUGH! THIS PLACE SHOULD BE CONDEMNED! IT'S LIKE ONE OF THOSE TV SHOWS ABOUT **HOARDERS**!

WHAT A WEIRD PLACE. DID YOU SEE THE WAY THE ANIMALS WERE **GRINNING**?

EEEEEEE

THAT NIGHT GREG GABARDINE, THE AMBULANCE DRIVER, TOLD HIS FAMILY ABOUT HIS DAY...
YOU SHOULD HAVE SEEN THIS PLACE! IT WAS LIKE A PIG STY!
AND HE'S GOT A "HOUSEKEEPER," IF YOU CAN BELIEVE THAT.

SHE WASN'T THERE, BUT I GUESS SHE'LL TAKE CARE OF THE PETS.
THERE ARE PETS?

A CAT AND A DOG. THEY WERE WEIRD TOO. IT ALMOST LOOKED LIKE THEY WERE **GRINNING** AT US.

I DIDN'T KNOW THERE WAS A CABIN IN THOSE WOODS.

I DIDN'T EITHER, ENID. IT'S AT THE END OF A LONG DIRT DRIVEWAY, JUST PAST GUNGY SWAMP.

8

People Will Talk

With Frank gone, the house was strangely quiet.

I put on the TV, but it just made me feel cranky. *Stupid commercials!*

About ten o'clock the phone rang. Trotter and I stared at it. The phone had never rung before. Not once.

Brringg, brringg.

"Should we answer it?" Trotter asked.

"Maybe it's Frank," I said. "Maybe it's the hospital!"

Trotter picked up the receiver in his teeth and put it on the shelf.

I knew what to say:

"Frank Mole's residence, housekeeper speaking." (You can learn a lot from old movies on television.)

It was Walt from the grocery store.

"I heard Frank was taken sick," he said. "Is he gonna be okay?"

"They took him to the hospital," I said. "But you can send out a bag of dried dog food and a case of cat food. And put it on the bill, as usual."

"It must be hard keeping house for Frank," Walt said, dragging out the conversation. "I hear the place is a . . . uh . . . kind of cluttered. Maybe you could use a mop and some cleaning powder, huh? Give it a good cleaning while he's away?"

I looked around, remembering the ambulance humans' reactions to the place. They had said it "oughta be condemned." And they implied that it smelled bad, too.

"All right," I said. "You can send those, too. And some of those big plastic bags like we used to have at the L — I mean at the last place I worked." (I almost said "at the Lab!")

Trotter put the phone back, leaving a smear of saliva all over it.

"Did you hear that?" I demanded. "Those people who took Frank away must have told Walt about how dirty this place is. It's probably all over town!"

"What's wrong with it?" asked Trotter sniffing the air. "I like it."

"At the lab they were always washing. Remember all those buckets and mops and that antiseptic smell? But here, nothing ever gets washed!"

"That why I like it," Trotter said. "It's casual!"

"Hmmm. Let's take a look at one of those shows the woman mentioned. What *are* hoarders, anyway?"

I put on the House Channel and scrolled down through the program guide.

"Here's one!" I cried. "*Hoarding Horrors.* It's on at 2:30."

I left the House Channel on, and we watched *Remake Your Neighbors' Yard, Buy to Sell, Get Green, Handy Houseman, Make it Work, Are We Living Yet*, and finally *Hoarding Horrors.*

They took a place that looked like ours, except it was much worse (I mean, Frank didn't clean much, but at least you could still see the floor!), threw everything in a big dumpster, washed the toilet with a toothbrush, painted all the walls, and got new furniture. Then everybody said, "Oh, wow," and hugged and the show was over.

I said, "We could do that."

Trotter said, "Do what?"

I said, "Give the house a makeover. I mean, just look at this mess! There are mouse droppings on the counter, and the phone is all slobbery. The mattress stinks. These old magazines are a fire hazard. Everything has got to go!"

"Uh . . . I don't think it's so bad. Me and Frank, we like it like this."

"Nonsense," I said.

"Do you realize we can order from other places besides Walt's? I don't know why I never thought of it before! We just have to find the number in the phone book and call them up and tell them what we want and give them the credit card number, like when Frank ordered his *Squadron* magazine!

"The first thing to do is to order the dumpster. You have to do it, Trotter, because you sound more like a Frank."

I was already pawing through the telephone book, looking for *Dumpster Rental*. And there they were — three different companies that rented dumpsters. They bring it and you fill it up and they take it away. Just like that!

The ambulance people had left Frank's wallet on the desk after taking out his health insurance cards. Luckily his credit card was still in it.

I punched in the phone number, because Trotter's paws are too big.

"Tell them we want to rent a dumpster," I said.

"We want to rent a dumpster," Trotter said into the phone. Then to me, "They want to know what size?"

"What size? How do I know what size? Tell them it's about the size of a car, like the one we saw on TV."

"Cash-on-delivery or card?" Trotter asked me.

"Card, of course. Give them the number. Here it is. I'll read it to you, and you can repeat it to them."

We gave them the address and told them to come all the way down the driveway and leave the dumpster next to the truck.

After Trotter hung up the phone he said, "They want me to put my name — I mean Frank's name — on the truck so they're sure they have the right place. What does hen-pecked mean?"

"I don't know," I said. "Pecked by a chicken, I suppose."

Three days later we heard the noise of a big flatbed truck coming up the driveway, so we hid in the house. When a man came to peer in the window, Trotter gave a menacing, low growl, and the man hurried off in his truck. But he left the dumpster.

Trotter and I went out to look at it.

"It's pretty big," Trotter said.

"Good," I said. "Let's get started."

We figured out how to open the back of it, then went inside to begin collecting garbage.

I pulled a black plastic bag out of the box. Trotter helped me open it and held it while I swept everything off the counter.

"Uh, don't you think we should keep some spoons?" Trotter said.

"No," I laughed, pushing a pile of cracked dishes into the bag with a crash. "Everything goes, and we can order new ones!"

"Save the calendar!" Trotter cried, just as I was about to make a clean sweep of all the stuff on the refrigerator.

Then I thought of something. "Trotter, isn't a refrigerator supposed to keep food cold and fresh? I've never seen Frank open this one, have you? Let's see what's inside! Maybe there's something good to eat!"

Frank's fridge was not cold. And it did not contain anything edible. Instead it was full of old containers and dried up messes and even old books and magazines! And it smelled.

Trotter's nose wiggled back and forth.

"Mold," he said. "Dried meat. Something sweet."

"Yuck," I said. "It all needs to go, Trotter. *Everything*! We'll give it a good wash, and later we'll get it repaired. And then think of all the good food we can keep in it!"

It wasn't easy, but with a rope and a trolley from the back of Frank's truck we got the heavy stuff out.

The mattress — OUT!

Frank's smelly old clothes — OUT!

We saved the desk with the important papers, and Frank's wallet, and the telephone book for future orders, and the phone, and the TV, of course.

Trotter wouldn't throw out Frank's chair. "Where will he sit when he comes home?" he asked.

"We'll order a new one!" I said.

"Well, after the new one comes, *then* we can throw out the old one. Maybe." he said. "Not before."

And I couldn't budge him. Obviously, I couldn't move the chair by myself.

"Okay," I said, stuffing Frank's jacket into a bag.

"Hey!" Trotter pulled the jacket out again and sniffed it. "It smells like Frank," he said.

"That's why it has to go," I explained.

"No."

Trotter put his front legs into the sleeves. "It still gets cold, nights," he said. "This will come in handy."

"Ha ha!" I laughed. "Now you look just like Frank!"

The Spy

I WAS TALKING TO WALT WHILE HE WAS GRINDING OUR COFFEE. HE SAYS THAT HOUSEKEEPER OVER AT FRANK MOLE'S CABIN HAS ORDERED A **DUMPSTER!**

SOUNDS LIKE SHE'S GONNA CLEAN THE PLACE UP. IT SURE NEEDS IT.

I WONDER WHAT MR. MOLE WILL SAY ABOUT **THAT.** WALT SAYS HE'S QUITE A HERMIT— DOESN'T NORMALLY LET ANYBODY NEAR THE PLACE.

BUT HE SAYS THAT THE HOUSEKEEPER SOUNDS LIKE MORE THAN A MATCH FOR HIM.

WELL, THAT'S JUST GOSSIP. NONE OF OUR AFFAIR.

DO YOU THINK WE THREW OUT TOO MUCH STUFF?
NO, AND NOW WE CAN WASH THE FLOOR.

IT WILL TAKE A LOT OF SOAP TO GET THIS FLOOR CLEAN.
WOOD SOAP

I'M GLAD WE SAVED SOME OF FRANK'S OLD SHIRTS.

HERE, TROTTER, YOU CAN GET STARTED WITH THIS ONE.
SPLOP

NOW RUB IT AROUND TO PICK UP THE DIRT.
LIKE THIS?

AREN'T YOU GOING TO WORK ON THE FLOORS, TOO?
IN A MINUTE, TROTTER. I HAVE TO WATCH THIS SHOW. IT'S GIVING ME SOME GOOD IDEAS.

IF I WASN'T ON THE LAM I COULD BE A GUEST ON ONE OF THESE DECORATING SHOWS.

WHAT WAS THAT?
CLONK

A DELIVERY! IT'S THE NEW SHINGLES AND THE ROOFING NAILS. BUT I'D BETTER TAKE A LOOK AT THAT INVOICE.

HMMM. I HOPE THERE WILL BE ENOUGH IN THE BANK TO COVER ALL THIS.
INVOICE

WHILE YOU RINSE THE FLOOR I'LL HAVE ANOTHER LOOK AT OUR FINANCES.

LET'S SEE... PAINT, NAILS, THE LADDER, THE DUMPSTER ... WE MIGHT HAVE TO CUT BACK ON OUR SPENDING.

SEE THAT YOU PAY EVERYONE ON TIME.

NAH! FRANK WAS ALWAYS TOO CAUTIOUS.

LET'S SEE ... WE'LL NEED FURNITURE, AND SOME DISHES, AND SOME PLANTS FOR THE GARDEN...

AND SO...
YOU CAN HARDLY SEE OUT OF THESE WINDOWS.

A LITTLE MORE TO THE LEFT, PLEASE.

CAREFUL, YOU'RE DRIPPING.

IT'S STARTING TO LOOK A LOT BETTER. NOW IT'S TIME TO WORK ON THE OUTSIDE.

HOW DO THESE SHINGLES WORK? ARE THERE DIRECTIONS ON THE BOXES?

I HOPE WE HAVE ENOUGH NAILS. WE CAN'T AFFORD ANY MORE.
NAILS
NAILS

IT'S NOT GOING TO BE EASY CARRYING ALL THIS STUFF UP TO THE ROOF.

WAIT! I'VE GOT AN IDEA!

NOW I CAN CARRY THE HAMMER AND NAILS IN MY POCKETS.

1...2...3... PULL!

THERE IT IS, THEY'VE GOT A MAN FIXING THE ROOF.

WE CAN START WITH THIS CORNER.
IT WOULD BE SO NICE TO HAVE THUMBS.

OK, I CAN HOLD THE NAIL. CAN YOU SWING THE HAMMER?
I THINK SO.

OW!
BLAM

BE CAREFUL, TROTTER! THAT WAS MY PAW!
SORRY.

IT'S KIND OF HARD TO SEE WITH THIS HAT.

WELL, TAKE IT OFF THEN.

THAT'S NOT A MAN!

IT'S A DOG!

10

Vicroy

It was a perfect day. The roof was done, and my landscaping design was almost complete. Trotter was just finishing the hole for my new butterfly bush.

"It won't bloom until August," I said, "but then it will be covered with purple blossoms and attract a lot of butterflies. Won't that be pretty against the woodshed?"

Trotter dragged the bush over and pushed the root ball into the hole. I gave it a good shot of water, and Trotter filled in the hole. Then I sat back to admire our work while he rolled in the leftover dirt.

"Do you know, I never saw a live butterfly before we came here?" I said to Trotter. "I like butterflies, don't you?"

"Sure." He stood up and shook off the dirt.

"Here, let me help you with that," I said, picking up the hose.

"Hey!" Trotter jumped out of the stream of water and ran around in a circle before rolling again and gulping at the spray.

"Ha, ha! Woof!" Trotter ran in and out of the water, and we laughed

as I chased him around the yard with it. Until he stopped short and pointed at the forest, ears forward, nose twitching. He gave a low growl.

I dropped the hose. "What is it?" I whispered.

"Someone coming," he replied.

"Human?"

"No. Dog."

The leaves rustled and a familiar face poked through.

"Vilroy!"

"Hello, Trotter. Scarlett."

The dog in the bushes was known to us, but I did not feel happy to see him. Back at the lab, Vilroy had often been cast as a villain. He looked the part, too, with his evil narrow eyes, his sharp teeth, and his pointed ears. And Vilroy was not fond of Trotter.

Jealous and conniving, that's how I would describe Vilroy. And possibly dangerous.

Now he stepped forward and sat down beside my bearded irises.

"Nice place you've got here," he said, looking around. "Where's your human?"

"He . . . " Trotter started to answer, but I cut him off.

"He's away," I said simply.

Trotter tends to be very trusting and honest – not always the best idea when dealing with Vilroy.

"How have you been, Vilroy?" I asked. "I guess you took advantage of the open window at the lab, too?"

"That's right. I saw Trotter going out and figured I might as well make a run for it myself. Nothing much going for me in the film business," he added with a sideways look at Trotter.

"The hunting's been pretty good," he continued, "especially with all the baby animals being born in the spring."

He looked over at our newly painted and shingled house. "I wouldn't say no to a little rest and relaxation, though . . . maybe just until your human gets back?"

Trotter and I looked at each other.

"Uh . . . would you like some refreshment, Vilroy?" I asked politely. After all, he had probably had a hard few months, and we could deal with the question of his staying later on. "Some dried food or some canned ravioli?"

"Dried would be great," he replied. "I haven't had any real dog food since I left the lab. And maybe some of the water from that hose? But I'll take mine in a bowl, thanks."

He climbed onto the lawn chair we had gotten for Frank and leaned back with a loud sigh. "When did you say your human will be back?" he asked.

"We didn't say, but I expect him any day now." This was not strictly true. We hadn't heard anything from Frank since the ambulance took him away. We didn't even know if he was still alive! As a matter of fact, we were getting along all right without him, but if his return would get rid of Vilroy, I was all for it. And of course, he *could* return at any moment.

But Frank did not return, and Vilroy hung around day after day. He snooped, watching our every move. He shuffled through Frank's desk, opened the mail, and hogged the remote when we were watching TV.

Finally, as his stay dragged on, I suggested that he might want to do his share of the work.

"You know I would love to help, Scarlett," he whined, "but I have this nagging pain in my shoulder. I must have strained it when I was struggling to survive on my own. And I wouldn't want to make it worse! Could you just bring me a little more of that cooked chicken breast? Heated up with gravy, there's a dear, Scarlett."

I had had enough.

"You'll have to get it yourself, Vilroy. Trotter and I are busy."

"So . . . " snarled Vilroy, showing his sharp canines. "No longer the gracious hostess. Well, let me tell you something, Scarlett. I see how you use the telephone. You order whatever you want. Well, you can order a few things for me while you're at it. And if you don't, I just might make a little call myself. To Pafco Studios! 'Is this Pafco Studios?' I'll say. 'And are you still looking for a certain missing dog and cat? Name of Trotter and Scarlett? I happen to know where you can find them.'"

"You wouldn't!" I gasped.

"Why not?" Vilroy grinned. "If I don't get what I want . . ."

"You . . . you . . . snake!"

"Then you would have to leave your lovely home, wouldn't you?"

He smiled, and it was not a pleasant look. "Just get me the chicken, Scarlett, and then don't disturb me while I prepare a mental list of the things I want ordered. And by the way, I don't believe for one minute that there *is* a human! We'll stay here happily forever – just the three of us."

Happily! I hadn't been happy since the day he arrived!

So the spring passed into summer.

Vilroy demanded a swimming pool, and Trotter worked on the hole until his paws were bloody.

And Vilroy watched television from Frank's new chair and demanded that I buy him every other thing that was advertised.

Finally, when he demanded that I order the two thousand dollar massage chair, I told him we couldn't afford any more purchases.

"I can't keep up with the credit card payments as it is," I said.

"Shall I make my little phone call, then?" Vilroy threatened.

"If you do, *you'll* lose the house, too," I said. "And if we don't pay the bills, we'll lose it anyway. Frank told me what happens when you don't pay your bills. *They come after you!* So do what you want, Vilroy. I've had enough of your bullying!"

"Yeah, me too," said Trotter. "From now on, you can dig your own swimming pool hole. And I just might swim in it when it's done!"

Behind us, the television was droning on.

I almost missed it, but the familiar numbers caught my ear . . . *twenty-five, thirty-seven, fifty* . . . and I didn't even hear Vilroy's reply.

"Those are Frank's lucky numbers!" I cried.

"What?" said Vilroy.

"SHUSH!"

. . . unclaimed lottery ticket, bought last March twenty-first. There are only six weeks left for the winner to come forward . . .

"Check the calendar!" I said to Trotter. "March 21. See? It's circled. That's the day Frank went to get his last ticket — the day of the ambulance!"

"What? What's going on?" said Vilroy.

We ignored him.

"Frank went out to buy his ticket, remember?" I said to Trotter.

"But did he ever get to the store?" Trotter asked. "Or did he turn around and come home when he got sick?"

"This Frank that you've been talking about — you mean he's a real human? You weren't just trying to scare me off?" Vilroy asked.

"He wouldn't turn around on a lottery ticket day," I said to Trotter.

"I demand to know what's going on!"

"Oh, shut up, Vilroy!" Trotter said. "Look in his wallet, Scarlett."

I already had it in my paws. I took everything out.

"Here!" Trotter pounced on a piece of paper that had fluttered to the floor.

I looked at it eagerly. "Trotter!" I cried. "Now we can pay the . . . no wait. It's the wrong date. See?"

"What is it?" Vilroy asked, more politely that he had spoken in weeks.

"It's a lottery ticket." I dropped it into the wastebasket. "Frank always bought a lottery ticket on Friday. And it looks like he had the winning ticket on March twenty-first, because those were his numbers! But he must have had it with him when he was taken away."

"Or . . ." Trotter held up a paw.

"Or we threw it out with the trash," I said sadly.

"Or . . ." Trotter persisted. "it's still in the truck!"

We all three ran out to the truck and practically took it apart.

But we never found the ticket.

11

Thwack

VILROY, I THOUGHT YOU SAID YOU WOULD HELP PICK UP THE LEAVES ON THE DECK.
MAYBE LATER. MY SHOULDER IS BOTHERING ME.

OH, NEVER MIND. I'LL DO IT MYSELF.

CRICK

WHAT WAS THAT? A SQUIRREL?
NO, I SMELL HUMAN!

SPRONG

EEEEK!

HAHA! I'VE GOT HER!
STOP!
THRASH

HELP!
LET GO OF ME, YOU HORRIBLE DOG!

SHE WAS HIDING BEHIND THE BUSHES, TAKING PICTURES. SHE KNOWS!

SURE, I'VE KNOWN FOR A LONG TIME, BUT I HAVEN'T TOLD ANYONE.

WELL, IT'S VERY IMPORTANT TO US THAT YOU NEVER TELL ANYONE.

HAHAHA
HA

DON'T YOU KNOW ANYTHING? YOU CAN'T TRUST A HUMAN! SHE CAN'T LEAVE THIS PROPERTY!

WHAT DO YOU MEAN?

I'VE KILLED A DEER. A HUMAN CAN'T BE MUCH HARDER.

VILROY, LET HER GO!

WE'VE PUT UP WITH A LOT FROM YOU, VILROY, BUT THIS TIME YOU'VE GONE **TOO FAR**!

OH, REALLY? AND WHAT ARE YOU GOING TO DO ABOUT IT?

GRRRRRRR...
GRRRRRRR...

GRAH

GRAZZLE
GNAZZLE

WHAT'S THE MATTER, TROTTER? DID YOU CUT YOUR EAR?
PANT, PANT...

WELL, THAT WILL SOON BE THE **LEAST** OF YOUR PROBLEMS!

OOF!
ROLL
SPLAT

GRAHH

GNAGHH
GRRRR

LUNGE

?
HAI!

THWACK

OWOOOOO
SPLAT

THAT WASN'T FAIR! WHERE DID YOU LEARN KUNG FU?

YOU'D BETTER LEAVE NOW, VILROY, BEFORE I REALLY LOSE MY TEMPER!

OKAY, I'M GOING ...

BUT YOUR CABIN DAYS ARE OVER!

AS SOON AS I CAN GET TO A PHONE, I'M CALLING PAFCO.

I'M SORRY, SCARLETT. I SHOULD HAVE RESTRAINED MYSELF.
NO, YOU SHOULDN'T. YOU WERE GREAT!
WHO'S PAFCO?

12

Enid

I was stunned.

All of a sudden, Trotter — kind, gentle Trotter — had turned *violent!* And now horrible Vilroy was finally gone, but not before threatening us with exposure! He was going to call Pafco, and *we would have to leave our home!*

"YOOOWL!" A woeful animal cry rose up out of me.

Trotter gave me a startled glance, then joined in with a lonesome howl of his own, "OW OOOWOOO!"

The strange human girl started to back away from us.

Attracted by her movement, Trotter and I both stopped howling and turned to look at her.

She stood still. "I wasn't . . . I wouldn't . . . tell," she said softly.

"I've watched you before," she confessed. "But I never told *anyone!* I saw you on the roof, shingling. I thought he was a man." She gestured toward Trotter. "When I saw he was a dog, I couldn't believe my eyes. So I watched again, and again, whenever I could. You fixed up the house. You acted like people. And you *talk!* I didn't know that until today, when I got up close. It's so *awesome!* And . . . and then . . . that big dog wanted to kill me!"

And she burst into tears.

"OO OO OWOOOO!" Trotter howled in sympathy.

"BAW!" wailed the girl.

"All right," I finally said. "That's enough of that."

The girl wiped her arm across her face. "Sorry," she said, still sniveling. "I don't usually cry, but I *was* kind of frightened. Well, terrified, actually." She gave a few final sobs, then added, more calmly. "My name is Enid Gabardine. My dad drives the ambulance. And I'm sorry I caused a fight with your friend."

"FRIEND?" Trotter cried. "HA! We're glad to be rid of him!"

"Except now he'll telephone Pafco, and we'll be found out," I added.

"Who *is* Pafco?" Enid said. "Or is it a what?"

"Pafco Studios," I said. "They make movies, and we used to live there. It's where we were born and bred – in the lab."

"Scarlett was the star!" Trotter added.

"You mean the place where those animal robots escaped from?"

The girl opened her eyes wide.

"We are *not* robots," I said.

"*That's* why you can talk!" she whispered. "It said on TV that you were dangerous!" And she turned and ran.

Trotter easily caught up to her. He was not rough like Vilroy, but he convinced her to return.

"We just want to explain," I said, after she was sitting on the porch under Trotter's watchful eye. "Trotter and I are *not* dangerous," I continued. "We're sorry that Vilroy attacked you. Apparently he *is* dangerous. I always suspected he could be. But *none* of us are robots! We don't know why they said so on TV. What I *do* know, is that we do not want to go back to that place. Sloan Pafco is a tyrant! And he kept us locked up in cages. And gave us shots!

"Oh, how terrible!" she said. She reached over and patted Trotter on the head. He seemed to like it, but then he's a dog.

"We've been so happy here," Trotter said, leaning right up against her.

She put her arm around him, and they looked into each others' eyes.

So who is there to comfort me, now that I am being driven out of house and home? And I felt another yowl coming on, but I swallowed it. Yowling doesn't get you anywhere. Better to face facts.

"Maybe we *have* been happy here," I said. "But now we have to leave, and the sooner, the better."

"But where will you go?" Enid asked me.

Trotter's sad, dark eyes asked me the same thing.

"Into the woods," I said. "Like before. We'll find another place."

I thought about my first trip through the woods – *the snow and the cold . . . the unknown.* This time it should be a lot easier. "I just wish I had a map," I added.

"You can download one from the Internet," Enid said.

"What?"

"Google it. You know, do a computer search."

"Oh, I see. But we don't have a computer."

"I thought everybody had a computer. I mean . . well, I guess that doesn't apply to cats and dogs . . . at least . . . ."

"Frank didn't have a computer, either," I said in our defense.

"You mean Mr. Mole? My Dad took him to the hospital."

"Yes. Well, we don't know when or *if* he will return. But if he does," I added, walking toward the cabin, "he'll find the place in better condition than it was when he left it."

The other two followed me in. Everything was in its place. The rugs were soft and bright. The counters were clean. The walls glowed sunny yellow. There was a vase of blue flowers on the small table. And the warm rust tones in the curtains picked up the richness of the polished floorboards. I just wished I hadn't overspent on the credit card. Frank would not be happy about that.

Enid looked around. "It looks so nice in here!" she exclaimed. "I *love* it!"

"We love it, too," Trotter sighed.

"Scarlett!" he said. "Maybe Vilroy won't ever make that call! What do you think?"

"I think I don't want to take that chance. I don't want to wake up one morning back in a cage. So let's get going. Just take what you need to survive."

I hopped up on the desk.

Enid sat in Frank's chair. "I have a survival kit at home," she said. "It has bandages and salt tablets. And a knife. You might need a knife."

I shuffled through some of the unpaid bills. *What was I supposed to take, anyway? A knife, as Enid suggested? What about Frank's credit card? Or would that be stealing? What about my special blanket? Our new camera? Some of the photos of my garden?*

"I know!" Enid jumped up. "Why don't you come to my house?"

Trotter's ears perked up.

"That Vilroy doesn't know where it is," she added, "so he can't turn you in!"

I thought about it. *Could we be safe there?* I wondered. Enid seemed like a nice human. But . . .

"Do you live alone?" I asked her.

"Ha, ha, ha!" She flopped back on the chair, laughing. "I'm only a kid! I live with my mother and father."

"Well, I don't know," I said, disappointed. "I think the fewer humans that know about us, the safer we'll be."

Trotter's ears drooped again.

"Maybe, if you didn't talk in front of them, they would think you were ordinary pets," Enid said. "My father saw you before, you know. When he was here with the ambulance. He thought you were house pets then, but that you were strange because you smiled so much."

She demonstrated a toothy smile. "Ordinary pets don't usually smile like this when they're feeling friendly. Dogs wag their tails, and cats just close their eyes and purr, or rub up against you."

Trotter wagged his tail. I did not rub up against anyone.

"We wouldn't stay forever," I said slowly. "Just until we figured out where to go."

"And you could use my computer!" Enid cried. "To print out your map."

In the end, we took nothing but our food.

"I hope your parents will be glad to have us," I said as Trotter closed the door and peered into the cabin for the last time.

Enid stopped. She looked worried.

"What?" Trotter asked.

"I was forgetting," she said. "But the last time I asked her, my mother wouldn't let me have a pet. You two aren't really pets, I know – you're really more like friends. But my mother won't know that, will she? Maybe she won't let you stay! "

Now I was disappointed.

"Maybe she wouldn't mind if she knew we were just temporary," I suggested. "What if I wrote her a note? From Frank's housekeeper, which I am, by the way, so it's not lying. I'll say . . . "

I hurried inside again. I found some pink paper in a drawer, and picked up my favorite pen. "I'll say . . ."

To Enid's Parents –
I have to leave suddenly, so could you take care of Scarlett and Trotter temporarily? They are well-behaved animals. Thank you very much.
from Frank Mole's Housekeeper

Enid read the note. "Yes," she said. "That's good. They like to help their neighbors. I think it will work!"

We closed the door again and set off into the woods, pulling our wagon full of food.

As we trudged along. I said to Trotter, "I didn't know you were a kung fu fighter."

"I learned it at the lab," he said. "Pafco was training some of us for a movie. I just never had any occasion to use it before."

13

House Pets

TEMPORARILY?

I WONDER WHAT TEMPORARILY MEANS, EXACTLY. SIX DAYS? SIX MONTHS?

I LIKE TO HELP OUR NEIGHBORS, ENID, BUT I DON'T QUITE LIKE HAVING IT **SPRUNG** ON ME LIKE THIS.

WELL, I SUPPOSE YOU CAN KEEP THEM — FOR NOW.

BUT I WILL NOT HAVE A DOG LIVING IN THE HOUSE!

FIND AN OLD BLANKET FOR A BED AND TAKE HIM OUT TO THE CHICKEN COOP.

I'M SORRY ABOUT THIS, TROTTER. IF I HAD KNOWN YOU WERE COMING WE COULD AT LEAST HAVE CLEANED IT UP A LITTLE.

OH, DON'T WORRY ABOUT ME. JUST TREAT ME LIKE A NORMAL...

SHHH

NO TALKING! AND BE CAREFUL! WE'LL SEE YOU IN THE MORNING.
CLUCK.

I WONDER WHAT HAPPENED TO THE CHICKENS ?

VILROY PROBABLY ATE THEM.

WELL, TOMORROW IS ANOTHER DAY . . .

SCARLETT, I'M SORRY, BUT WE'LL HAVE TO KEEP YOUR FOOD IN THE LAUNDRY ROOM.

AND YOU BETTER NOT GET ANY CAT HAIR ON THE FURNITURE. MY MOTHER WOULDN'T LIKE IT.

IT ALMOST LOOKS AS IF THAT CAT IS ENJOYING YOUR SHOW, ENID.
HA HA!

I'LL BE IN THE OFFICE ALL DAY, ENID. KEEP THE CAT OUT OF YOUR FATHER'S STUDIO, AND TAKE THE DOG FOR A WALK LATER.
OK, MOM. I WILL.

YOU CAN COME IN MY ROOM NOW, SCARLETT. DAD WON'T BOTHER US.

AND I WANT TO SHOW YOU HOW TO USE MY COMPUTER.

WHAT DO YOU WANT TO LOOK UP FIRST?

LET'S SEE WHAT IT SAYS ABOUT SLOAN PAFCO!

THAT'S HIM!
CYBERPEDIA
SLOAN PAFCO

IT SAYS HERE THAT WHEN HE WAS YOUNG HE WAS A BRILLIANT SCIENTIST!

BUT HE WAS FIRED FROM THE UNIVERSITY WHERE HE WORKED FOR EXPERIMENTING ON ANIMALS.

WHAT KIND OF EXPERIMENTS?

LET'S SEE... IT SAYS HE WAS ARRESTED FOR TRYING TO MAKE A HUMKEY...

WHICH IS A CREATURE THAT IS HALF MONKEY AND HALF...
HUMAN!

LATER...
OH MY GOSH! WE'VE FORGOTTEN ABOUT TROTTER IN THE CHICKEN COOP!

THAT'S THE TROUBLE WITH COMPUTERS!

WHAT TOOK YOU SO LONG?

YOU SHOULD SEE THIS COMPUTER, TROTTER. YOU CAN LOOK UP ANYTHING.

WE'VE BEEN FINDING OUT A LOT ABOUT SLOAN PAFCO.

WE LEARNED THAT HE GOT IN TROUBLE FOR EXPERIMENTING WITH ANIMALS—MIXING SPECIES.

THAT WAS BEFORE HE GOT INTO THE MOVIE BUSINESS?
RIGHT.

I'D LIKE TO FIND OUT MORE ABOUT HIS FILM-MAKING AND THE SO-CALLED **ANIMAL ROBOTS**!

UH-OH, HERE COMES MY DAD. NO MORE TALKING!

LOOK AT THAT CAT! GOING FOR A WALK WITH YOU AND THE DOG!

WHAT DID YOU SAY HIS NAME WAS?
TROTTER.

LOOKS PART RETRIEVER. WANT TO PLAY FETCH, BIG FELLOW?

I'LL JUST TAKE OFF HIS LEASH, DAD.

(RUN AFTER THE STICK WHEN HE THROWS IT AND BRING IT BACK TO HIM.)

OKAY.
COUGH COUGH

THAT'S A NASTY COUGH YOU'VE GOT, ENID.

ROWF

ATTA BOY!

NEXT MORNING:
OKAY, MY PARENTS ARE AWAY THIS MORNING, SO YOU CAN COME IN FOR A LITTLE WHILE.

BUT DON'T SIT ON THE FURNITURE.
OKAY, OKAY.

YESTERDAY WE RESEARCHED SLOAN PAFCO. NOW LET'S SEE WHAT IT SAYS ABOUT HIS **FILMS**!

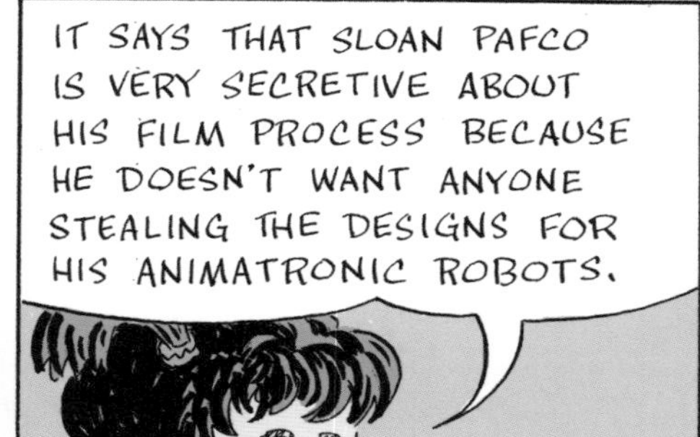
IT SAYS THAT SLOAN PAFCO IS VERY SECRETIVE ABOUT HIS FILM PROCESS BECAUSE HE DOESN'T WANT ANYONE STEALING THE DESIGNS FOR HIS ANIMATRONIC ROBOTS.

AND IT SHOWS A PICTURE OF ONE OF HIS ROBOTS.
THAT'S **ME**!

SLOAN PAFCO INSERTING A BATTERY PACK INTO ONE OF HIS FILM ROBOTS.

ENID, LOOK AT MY BACK! DO YOU SEE ANY PLACE FOR BATTERIES ?
NOPE.

THIS MAKES ME SO MAD! I AM NOT A ROBOT!

OWOOOO!

OWOOOOOOO!

ENID, WHAT IS GOING ON HERE?

14

The Deal

Enid's mother (Mrs. Gabardine) stood in the doorway. *How much had she overheard?*

She began quietly, but her voice rose with each sentence. "I thought we had agreed that the dog would stay outside, Enid. At *least* until we could give him a bath. He could be harboring fleas and ticks and who knows *what* all! Why, I wouldn't be surprised if he had *WORMS!*"

Trotter hung his head and slunk, ears drooping, into the far corner.

Mr. Gabardine poked his head in. "What's up?" he asked.

"I knew these animals would cause trouble," his wife replied.

"Nothing serious, I'm sure," Mr. Gabardine said. "He's a good dog, aren't you, Trotter? We had a nice game of fetch yesterday, Trotter and I," he explained to Mrs. Gabardine.

She gave an angry little snort in reply.

I dropped silently to the floor and slipped under the bed.

Enid's mother looked around the room. "Where are your friends, Enid? I hope there's no reason for them to hide from me."

Does she mean me? I wondered. But I stayed put.

"What friends?" Enid asked.

"I'm sure I heard talking in here, just a moment ago, before those animals of Frank Mole's began making such a racket!"

Enid squirmed in her chair. "I was just talking to Scarlett and Trotter," she said.

"Why the guilty look then, Hon?" Her father squeezed past his wife and came into the room.

Clomp, clomp. I got a good look at Mr. Gabardine's big shoes as he approached Enid's desk. Human clothing is somewhat strange.

"You remember our open-door Internet policy, right? So suppose you show us just what it is you've been doing. It's for your own safety, you know. With so many dangerous frauds online, you can't believe half of what you read."

How true, I thought. *Just look at those false Pafco robots!*

"I was just googling some stuff," Enid said to her father.

"What is it, Greg?" asked Enid's mother, following him into the room.

"Pafco Studios . . . animatronics . . . films . . . robots. It all looks fairly innocent to me. Nothing to worry about. Maybe our Enid is contemplating a future in the movie business. Is that it, Hon?"

"Let me see that," Enid's mother said.

"Why, that looks just like Mr. Mole's cat!" she cried. "And Pafco Studios . . . now, why does that sound so familiar? Isn't that the place that was all over the news last winter? With the animal robots? Move over, Enid." And she reached over Enid and began scrolling through the images.

Enid let her mother have the chair. "They aren't robots," she said.

Her parents weren't listening.

"Look at this, Greg. It says . . ."

Enid raised her voice. "THEY AREN'T ROBOTS!"

Both parents turned to look at her.

"Those pictures have been photoshopped," she said. "I could explain," she added, "but it's somebody else's secret, and I promised not to tell."

I could see where this was going. I've watched kids' movies on TV. I know it's not a good idea for them to keep secrets from their parents. Besides, there was that picture of me right there on the computer. I crawled out and stood beside Enid.

"It's all right," I said to her. "We had better tell them."

Her mother sucked in her breath with a whooshy little squeak.

"Who said that?" she said sharply, looking around the room.

"They're transgenics," Enid explained. "We've just been reading about it. Scarlett and Trotter are victims of Sloan Pafco's illegal activities! He's been developing animals with human genes so they can speak and act in his so-called animated films. But it's illegal, so he makes everyone believe they're robots. Right, Scarlett?"

"I couldn't have put it better myself," I said.

"I never really liked that Mr. Pafco," Trotter added, coming forward.

"Stop it, Enid!" Mrs. Gabardine cried, her voice high and squeaky. "I don't know how you're doing this, but I don't find it one bit funny."

"It's not a trick. And they can do more than just talk. They can read and write and use the telephone. They even cleaned up Mr. Mole's house and fixed the roof, and Scarlett was Mr. Mole's *housekeeper!*"

"Do you know how he is, by the way?" I asked.

Mrs. Gabardine sank down on the bed. "Do something, Greg," she said weakly.

"Let's hear her out," he replied. "Go ahead, Enid."

It took the parents awhile, but by the time they had heard the whole story — about the lab, and our escape, and our time with Frank, and what Enid had seen — they seemed more ready to accept the fact that it was really us speaking.

"All I can say is, this Sloan Pafco operation had better be investigated by the proper authorities," Mr. Gabardine announced.

"He doesn't sound like a very nice man, but why is it *illegal?*" Enid asked. "I think it would be great if there were *more* talking animals!"

"Well, it's important for anyone who tampers with nature to be very cautious; to take into account many points of view; to listen to reason and experience. Look at it this way — in order to come up with a Trotter and a Scarlett, Pafco must have worked through many mistakes. And that's something I'd rather you didn't think about too deeply, Enid."

Which of course is just what *does* make you think about it. *Those*

strange noises from the locked rooms at the lab. The trucks making pickups at midnight. Some sad-eyed, silent workers. Were they all Sloan Pafco mistakes?

Mr. and Mrs. Gabardine very kindly invited us to move into their guest room, and we gratefully accepted.

Then they made a lot of phone calls — some to a lawyer-friend of theirs and some to various government officials — all of which eventually resulted in an important meeting at PAFCO studios.

Trotter and I were invited, but not Enid. I didn't want to go either, but Mrs. Gabardine said she thought it was important for the others to hear my story. And she promised that they wouldn't leave me there.

So I went, and I told my story.

The whole time I was talking, Mr. Pafco glared at me like he wanted to wring my neck. Fortunately there were two men in uniform standing beside him. When I said, "So then we googled Sloan Pafco on the computer . . ." his face turned purple and he started to rise out of his chair, but one of the uniformed men put a firm hand on his shoulder, and he sat down again very quickly.

When it was his turn to talk, he began, "You should *thank* me! My achievements have been great. So what if I had a few mistakes along the way? The results, well, you can see for yourself." He gestured toward me and Trotter. "If I have profited financially, it has been justly deserved."

Deserved? You act outside the law. You make us part-human, then you confine us and make us work for you. You deserve profits? If I weren't so polite, I would have puked up my breakfast.

Afterwards there was a tour of the lab. The men in uniform made Mr. Pafco open the door to the "No Admittance" area, and the visiting humans filed in. But Trotter and I chose to visit with some of our old friends instead.

It had been a stressful event. I fell asleep during the final discussions, but Mr. Gabardine woke me up to ask me if I would be willing to complete the filming of *Scarlett on the Run* (our unfinished movie) under the supervision of an animal and human rights oversight committee.

Of course I said no. "I'm through with acting," I said.

"Don't decide until you hear us out, Scarlett," the Gabardines' lawyer pleaded. "Keep in mind that once Sloan Pafco is brought to justice, the story of what he has been doing will become public, and any film produced by the studio will undoubtedly be extremely successful."

"But not without Scarlett!" Trotter interjected.

"Just so," the lawyer said. "And therefore, we have drawn up a contract whereby the actors, like yourself, will receive royalties from box office receipts, and, most importantly, the bulk of the profits will be used to finance the building of a self-run sanctuary for all those who have been, uh, conceived here, successfully and otherwise."

They were all looking at me.

I spoke to Mrs. Gabardine. "You said you wouldn't leave me here," I reminded her.

"No, of course not," the lawyer answered for her. "Filming won't start right away. We still have one or two things to arrange. After that it *would* be more convenient if the actors were on site. But I'm sure something else could be arranged, if necessary."

"I won't be locked in," I said cautiously.

"No, no, of course not. All the locks will be removed. And the oversight committee will be looking out for your interests."

Trotter was willing, so I agreed also, and we signed the papers.

15

The Return

AFTER THE MEETINGS WE WENT BACK TO THE NICE GUEST ROOM AT ENID'S HOUSE.

THE GABARDINES DIDN'T NEED MUCH HELP IN THE KITCHEN.
NO, THANK YOU, SCARLETT.

TROTTER GREW QUITE GOOD AT FETCHING A BALL.
THIS IS WAY MORE FUN THAN THE EXERCISE WHEEL!

THEN ONE DAY:
SCARLETT, WHY DON'T YOU AND TROTTER WALK BACK TO THE CABIN WITH ENID? YOU CAN MAKE SURE EVERYTHING IS OKAY THERE.

YES, I WOULD LIKE THAT.

I HOPE NOTHING HAS HAPPENED TO IT.
WHAT IF VILROY CAME BACK AND WRECKED EVERYTHING?

JUST LOOK AT THOSE COBWEBS! ENID, WOULD YOU GIVE ME A HAND DUSTING?

AND, TROTTER, WOULD YOU MIND CHECKING THE MAILBOX?

I THINK WE COULD USE SOME FRESH AIR!

THERE! THAT LOOKS BETTER!

RONFA NONFA LOMF!
WHAT?

I SAID, "THERE'S A LOT OF MAIL!"
SPLAT

UH-OH!
THIS ONE SAYS "PAST DUE."

SOMEONE'S COMING.
HONK

BUT WE HAVEN'T ORDERED ANYTHING.

IT'S MOM AND DAD.

AND FRANK!

WHAT'S GOING ON HERE? WHERE'S ALL MY STUFF?

SCARLETT AND TROTTER CLEANED IT UP FOR YOU. DOESN'T IT LOOK NICE?

WE EXPLAINED EVERYTHING TO HIM, BUT I'M NOT SURE HE UNDERSTANDS.

I UNDERSTAND, ALL RIGHT! FILLING MY HOUSE WITH A LOT OF USELESS FROU-FROUS!

AND WHO'S PAYING FOR IT? THAT'S WHAT I'D LIKE TO KNOW.

WHAT? AN UNPAID BALANCE OF $10,561.22!!!

NOW, MR. MOLE, DON'T GET OVEREXCITED.
I'VE BEEN ROBBED!

LOOK, FRANK, WE SAVED YOUR OLD JACKET.
GIVE ME THAT!

WHAT'S THIS IN THE POCKET?
THOSE ARE SOME NAILS FROM WHEN WE PUT ON A NEW ROOF.

I DIDN'T NEED A WHOLE NEW ROOF! A CAN OF ROOFING TAR WOULD HAVE FIXED IT FINE!

WHAT ELSE IS IN HERE? MORE BILLS?

JUST AN OLD LOTTERY TICKET.

POUNCE

WHAT IS IT?

MARCH 21! AND THE NUMBERS ARE RIGHT!

FRANK! THIS IS A WINNING LOTTERY TICKET, AND YOU STILL HAVE TEN DAYS TO CLAIM IT!

16

Sanctuary

After my escape, I had thought I would never willingly return to Pafco Studios to make another movie. Yet there I was, singing and dancing and taking direction from a chastened Mr. Pafco.

And, as promised, the oversight committee was on hand to make sure we were well-treated. They even banned the use of energy shots.

Vilroy had heard that we were filming again, and he showed up to resume his role as the villain.

"You know, Scarlett," he said to me, showing his teeth in a false smile, "I never *really* planned to call Pafco and rat on you. It was just a threat."

"Whatever," I said. "It's past history now." And I walked away.

I was glad when my work on the movie was finished. It went to editing, and Sloan Pafco went to trial for illegal use of human genetic material.

I stayed on at the Studio while the sanctuary was being built. The Gabardines had offered their guest room, but it just didn't feel like home. And besides, there was nothing to do there.

I didn't want to sleep in my old cage, though, so I set up a pillow in a corner of the stage. But that wasn't really like home either – not like our old cabin. We didn't hear anything from Frank.

The movie was a huge box-office success, so the sanctuary turned out to be quite fancy. There was a large clubhouse with games and restaurants. And a quiet residential area with a peaceful park that was popular with the feline members.

We each had our own little house, called a pod, and a mini-cart. Everything was new and shiny. There were grounds-keepers. We had our own bank, and you could order in.

So why is it, I wondered as I twittered the mah jong tiles, *that I'm not more, well . . . happy?*

After the game I drove my mini-cart over to Trotter's pod.

He wasn't home.

"He's probably at the arcade," I said to myself, and I left him a note.

He came over the next morning looking a little bloodshot in the whites of his eyes.

"How have you been, Trotter?" I asked him. "Are you getting enough sleep?"

"Sure," he said. "Couldn't be better. I broke the *Deathly Dragons* record, and now me and the boys are talking about putting in some slot machines!" He yawned. "How about you, Scarlett?"

"I don't know," I replied. "I was thinking about the old days. Remember when the ambulance people came, and we tried to act like happy, normal pets?"

"Ha, ha! We weren't very good at it. But we fooled them anyway."

"And remember when we told Frank he had the winning lottery ticket?"

Trotter smiled, thinking back. "He didn't believe you, at first," he said.

"No. He didn't know how to be not grouchy."

"Ha, ha! Frank was always grouchy."

“But then,” I said, “He did that little dance, waving his ticket and going, ‘Wahoo!’”

“Yeah.”

“I sent him a copy of *Scarlett on the Run,* but I never heard anything back,” I said.

“Too busy watching the game,” Trotter guessed.

“Well, he must be happy, anyway, with all that money he won. He probably even has a new housekeeper.”

“Yeah, and a gardener and a chauffeur. He probably even moved to a new house — a big mansion.” Trotter took a few sloppy laps of his warm milk. “With normal housepets,” he added.

17

Scarlett on the Run

BUT FRANK HAS NOT SQUANDERED HIS WINNINGS ON A MANSION AND SERVANTS. IN FACT, HE IS STILL LIVING IN THE SAME OLD CABIN...

ON A REMOTE ISLAND IN THE SOUTH PACIFIC...

THUNKA THUNK

OOOOOAAH

SCARLETT DANCES TO APPEASE THE VOLCANO GOD.

LOOK! THE LAVA FLOW HAS STOPPED!

SCARLETT MUST DANCE TO THE DEATH AS A SACRIFICE TO THE VOLCANO GOD!

DANCE, SCARLETT, DANCE!

IT'S ALL OVER, YOUR MAJESTY.
GOOD! THROW HER INTO THE VOLCANO!

OH, I GET IT! THEY ONLY THREW IN THE PLANK! SCARLETT IS SAFE!

SCARLETT, THE CHIEF CAN NEVER KNOW THAT YOU LIVE!

YOU MUST LEAVE THE ISLAND FOREVER!

FAREWELL!
GOOD-BYE!

SNAP

WHERE AM I ?

CALIFORNIA, MA'AM – THE LAND OF GOLD! AND I'M ABOUT TO CASH IN MY NUGGETS!

KONK

HA HA HA!
HELP! HELP!

HAHA! YOU'RE A SAUCY ONE!

LET ME GO!

OUCH! YOU LITTLE VIXEN! GO THEN! YOU'LL NEVER MAKE IT ON YOUR OWN...

LOOK AT THE POOR DANCER. TOSS HER A PENNY, TOMMY.

I CAN MAKE YOU A STAR, HEH, HEH...

...ANOTHER BAG OF NUGGETS! BUT AFTER I CASH IN, I'M GOING TO FIND THAT POOR CAT...

SCARLETT TRAVELS THE GLOBE, BESET BY VILLAINY, FIRE, EARTHQUAKE, AND FLOODS. SHE DANCES IN THE STREETS TO EARN A FEW COINS, ALL THE TIME DREAMING OF HER ISLAND HOME.

SCARLETT! IS IT REALLY YOU?

I HAD TO RETURN, WHATEVER THE DANGER!

THERE IS NO DANGER! THE OLD CHIEF JUST DIED!

SCARLETT AND TROTTER LIVED TOGETHER HAPPILY IN A SMALL HOUSE OF WOOD AND STRAW.

TROTTER LEARNED TO PLAY THE UKULELE.

SCARLETT TAUGHT DANCING TO THE ISLAND CHILDREN.

AFTER MANY YEARS SHE BECAME ILL AND TOOK TO HER BED.
I FEEL A LITTLE TIRED.

IS THERE ANYTHING I CAN GET FOR YOU?

YES. TAKE ME OUTSIDE SO I CAN SEE THE SKY ONE MORE TIME.

LOOK! THE CLOUDS ARE DANCING!

SCARLETT! DON'T GO!

AHHHHHHHHHHHHHH
The End

CLICK

SNIFFLE

HONK

KNOCK
KNOCK

GO AWAY! I'M NOT HOME!

OPEN UP, FRANK! IT'S US—SCARLETT AND TROTTER.

SCARLETT? TROTTER?

JUST A MINUTE... AHEM... AHEM...

WELL, WHADDA YOU WANT?

(SAME OLD FRANK.)

THE GABARDINES BROUGHT US OVER. WE WANTED TO VISIT YOU FOR FATHER'S DAY.

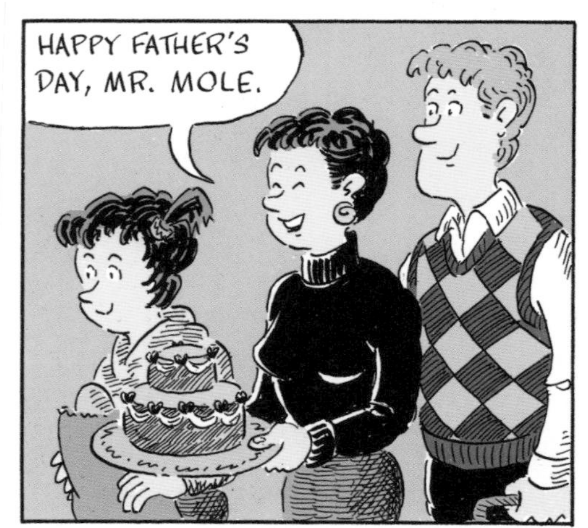
HAPPY FATHER'S DAY, MR. MOLE.

ME? BUT I'M NOT A FATHER.

WELL, YOU'RE THE CLOSEST THING WE'VE GOT.

BESIDES, WHO DOESN'T LIKE CAKE?

WE'LL HAVE OUR CAKE OUTSIDE ON THE PICNIC TABLE.
I'LL JUST PUT THESE DISHES TO SOAK.
WE CAN CLEAN UP LATER.

NOW JUST A BLOGGIN' MINUTE!

OUTSIDE! ALL OF YOU!

YOU TOO, CAT.

AND GIMME THAT CAKE!

WELL? WADDA YOU WAITING FOR? SIDDOWN!

HMPF!

WHOSE HOUSE IS THIS ANYWAY?

DID I FORGET ANYTHING?

I'VE GOT AN IDEA, MR. MOLE. WHY DON'T YOU **ADOPT** SCARLETT AND TROTTER?

OH, THEY WOULDN'T WANT TO MOVE BACK HERE. THEY'RE BIG MOVIE STARS NOW.

I LIVE ALONE, AND THAT'S HOW I LIKE IT.

BUT WE EVEN BROUGHT OUR **SUITCASES**.

WHAT? YOU MEAN YOU WANT TO STAY?

WHEN'S THE LAST TIME YOU COOKED YOURSELF A GOOD MEAL—WITH VEGETABLES?

YOU NEED US, FRANK.

AND BESIDES, WE LIKE YOU!

YOU... LIKE ME?

THEY LIKE ME!

AND SO...
I MISSED YOU, CAT.

PURRR
SEE YOU SOON.
The End

ANNE of GREEN BAGELS
Susan Schade
Jon Buller

WATCH OUT FOR PAPERCUTZ™

Welcome to the awesome SCARLETT graphic novel by Susan Schade and John Buller, from Papercutz (or maybe in this case, it should be PaperCATz?), those cat-lovers dedicated to publishing great graphic novels for all ages. I'm Jim Salicrup, the Editor-in-Chief, and president of the Scarlett fan club, Greenwich Village Chapter.

SCARLETT is something a little different for Papercutz, but that's a good thing. Papercutz, as I just noted, is dedicated to publishing great graphic novels (although we're also publishing NICKELODEON MAGAZINE too!), but is SCARLETT really a graphic novel? The first chapter sure starts out as a graphic novel, but something happens in chapter two—it turns into a more traditional chapter book, with the story being told in prose with illustrations. I'm not sure why the authors decided to tell their story this particular way, but I know I like it. After all, where are the rules that says you can't alternate from a graphic novel to an illustrated prose novel within the same book? I'll tell you where—there aren't any such rules. For those who crave consistency, may I remind you of the wonderful words of Ralph Waldo Emerson, who said "A foolish consistency is the hobgoblin of little minds." Fortunately, I'm thankful that the folks who follow Papercutz are very wise and have great big minds. We loved this graphic novel/illustrated novel hybrid so much, we already have another one lined up for you from the same creative team of Susan Schade and Jon Buller. And if you thought SCARLETT's tale was a tad unusual, wait till you meet ANNE OF GREEN BAGELS...

On her first day at her new school, Anne is saddled with the nickname *Anne of Green Bagels*, thanks to the health-food sandwich her grandmother has made her for lunch. Can things get any worse? Already her father has left home to try out his newest crackpot invention, the Pedestrian Mobile Home, and her mother has moved them from New Mexico to the cookie-cutter community of Megatown. Then she meets Otto, who shares her interest in music and in her favorite TV show, The Blimptons. Together they prepare to enter the school talent show with an original composition — Wolfman Stomp. When Anne sees the drawings in a childhood notebook of her father's, she wonders — could it be that *he* was the real inventor of the Blimptons? And can she somehow get him to come home and claim the credit he deserves?

And that doesn't even mention the flying green bagels! We're betting if you enjoyed SCARLETT, that you'll love ANNE OF GREEN BAGELS, coming your way soon from Papercutz! Until then, be sure to write us and let us know what you thought of SCARLETT, and if you loved SCARLETT, be sure to tell your friends!

Thanks,

Jim

STAY IN TOUCH!

EMAIL: salicrup@papercutz.com
WEB: papercutz.com
TWITTER: @papercutzgn
FACEBOOK: PAPERCUTZGRAPHICNOVELS
MAIL: Papercutz, 160 Broadway,
Suite 700, East Wing, New York, NY 10038

Other Great Titles From PAPERCUTZ™

And Don't Forget . . .

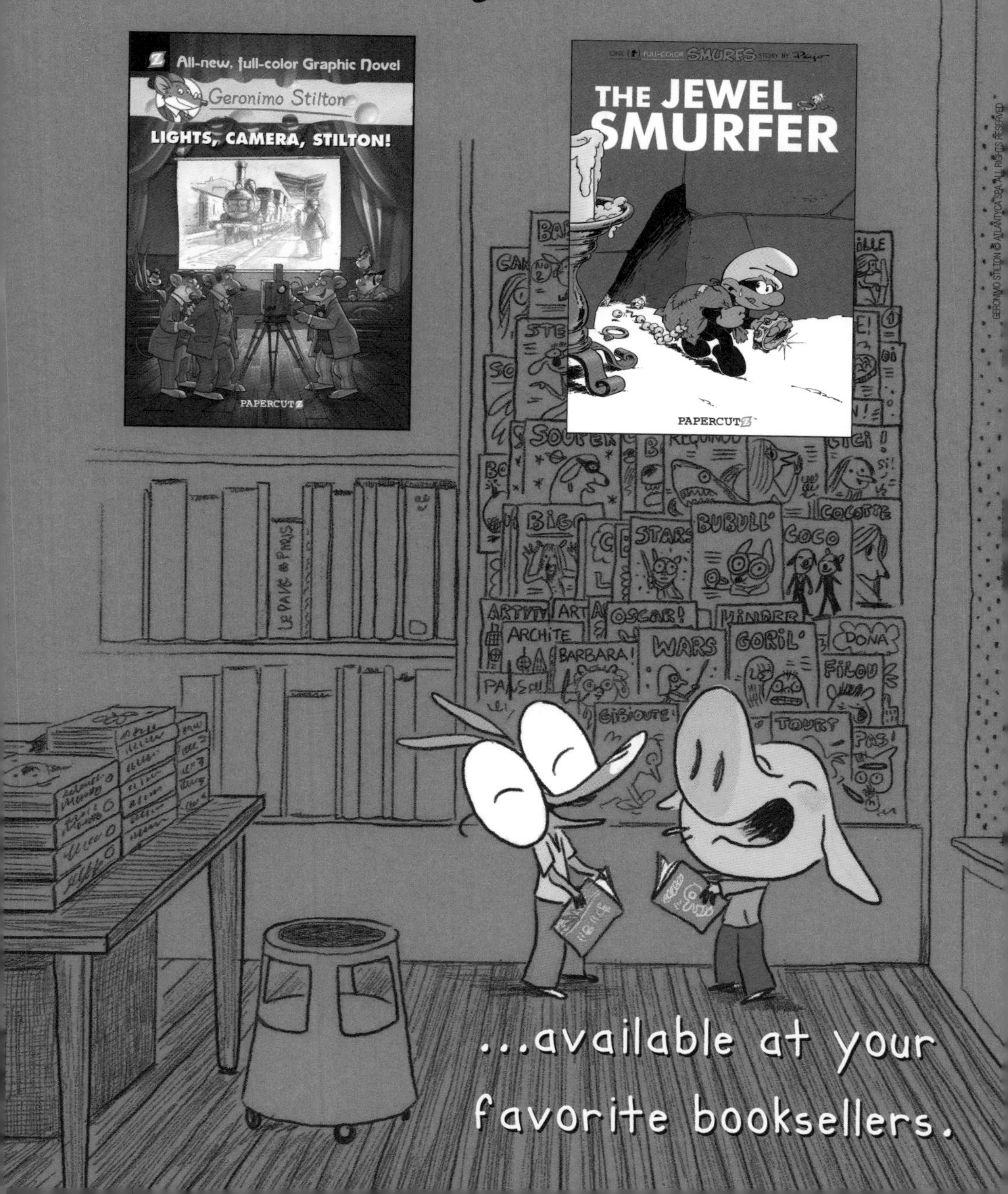